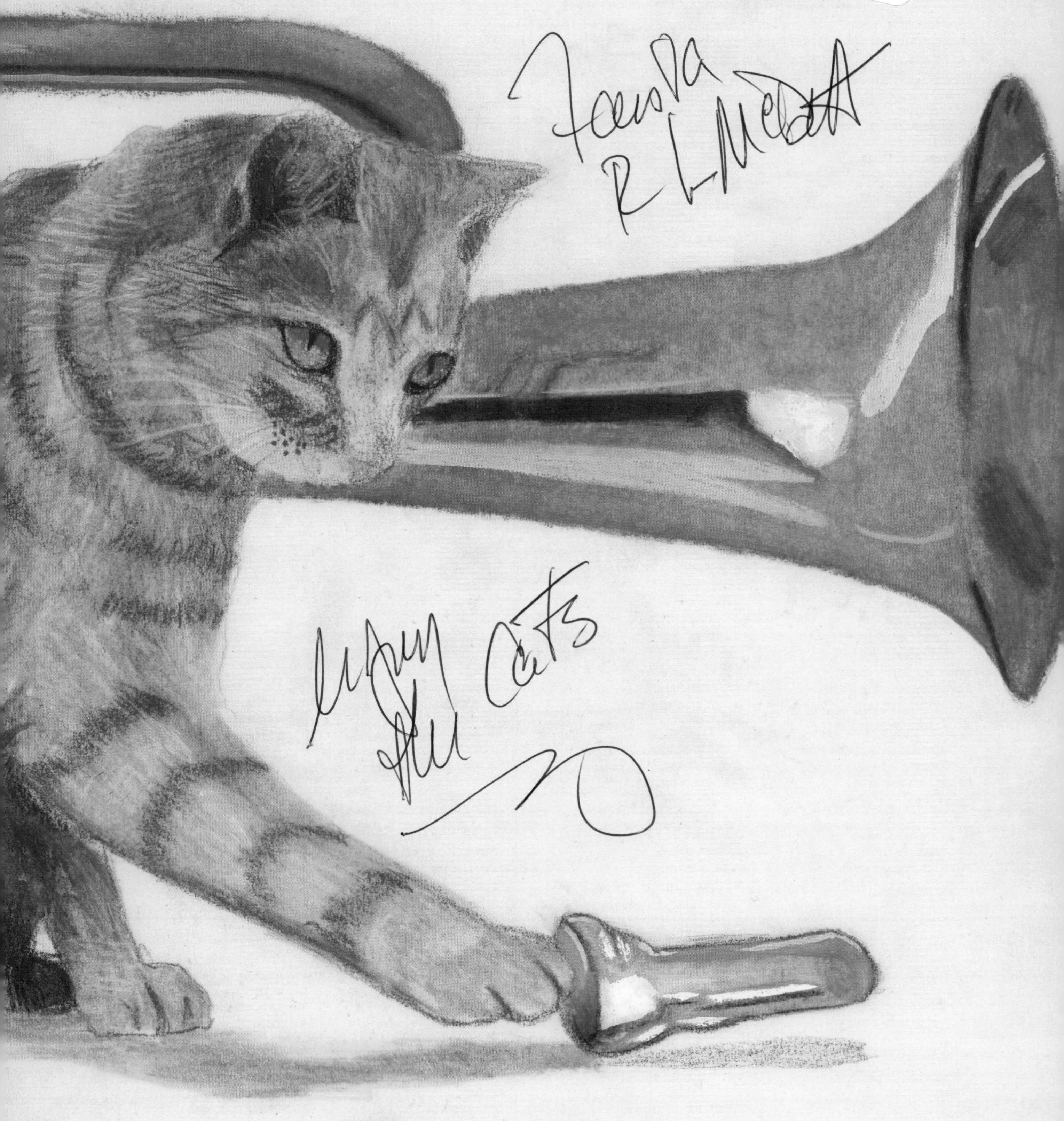

In loving memory of
Stephanie Marie and
Anthony John
who inspired their parents to write this book
for all children to enjoy.

Special thanks to Alan Reingold for patiently helping Joseph to become a skillful artist.

By Fausta R. L. and Michael J. McDermott
Illustrated by Joseph A. McDermott

The Concert Hall Cats

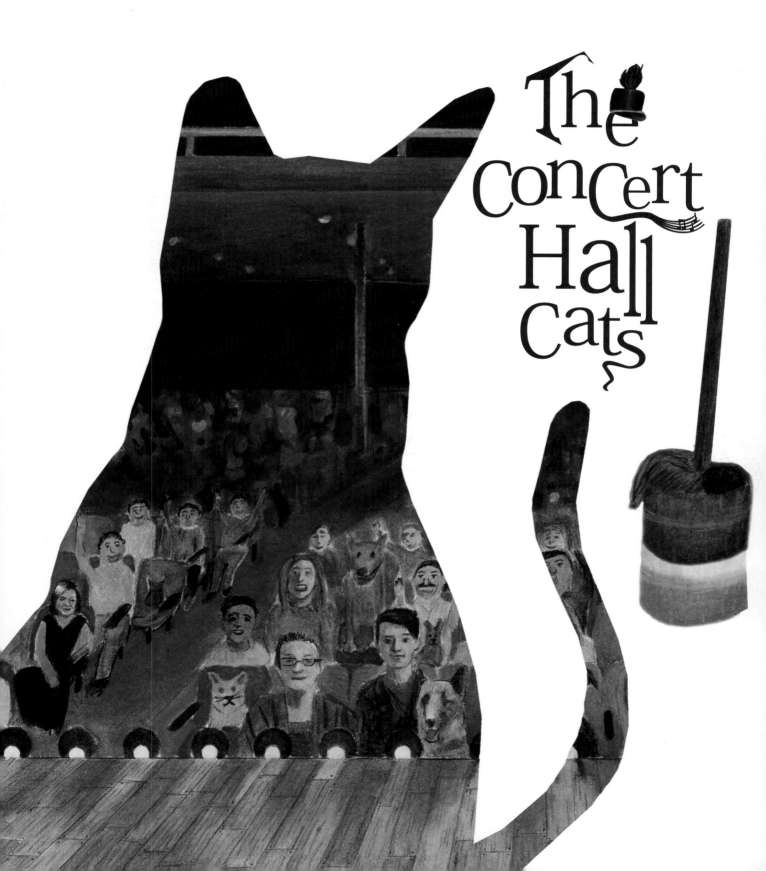

In the middle of a big city, Horatio the Cat lived in a majestic old concert hall with his wife, Sofia, and their playful kittens, Mary and Eddie.

Each day, when the warm rays of the sun poured through the stained-glass windows, the concert hall transformed into a kaleidoscope of dazzling, swirling colors. Mary and Eddie never tired of chasing the shimmering parade of color as the sun slowly rolled across the sky.

Sofia had made a cozy home in the attic, where the old musical instruments and orchestra uniforms were stored. She fashioned a warm bed for her kittens inside a big bass drum, which had one side missing. Serving as both pillow and blanket was a conductor's jacket that had once been bright red.

While Sofia quietly watched, the kittens would play for hours on the instruments stored in the attic. Trying to outdo each other, they made acrobatic leaps between two small drums. They would slide down the neck of the big cello and onto the xylophone, creating a whirlwind of music as they scampered across, laughing with joy as they landed on a pile of old uniforms.

Both kittens loved to prance on the old piano; each time they pounced on the keys, a wild assortment of musical notes would echo throughout the hall.

Eddie imagined that their drum was a pirate ship, and he was the brave captain fearlessly facing the perils on the rough, wild seas. Mary would sit in front of the big tuba and pretend it was a mysterious cave. She delighted in telling Eddie scary stories about the ghosts that lived inside.

Jimmy the Janitor lived alone in the basement and was very proud of how clean he kept the concert hall. He was always looking for windows to wash, floors to scrub, light bulbs to replace, and doors to fix.

As he worked, Jimmy enjoyed listening to the kittens playing in the attic. Each morning, he brought them a large bowl of milk to drink and wonderful treats to eat.

One morning, Jimmy noticed that little Eddie was limping. The kitten had hurt his tiny paw falling off the piano, so the thoughtful janitor rushed to find a bandage. To show his appreciation, Horatio jumped into Jimmy's strong arms and licked his face.

In the past, many people had come to enjoy the music played in the concert hall. But huge shopping malls and movie theaters had opened across town, and most people didn't even know that the hall was still open. Yet, every Friday evening, the orchestra performed on the big stage. With tubas, violins, trumpets, saxophones, and all the other instruments, the musicians created the most beautiful and inspiring music— though only a few people still came to the concerts.

Each Friday, Horatio and his family would carefully walk across the beams high above the stage and sit in their favorite place above the seats. Tilting their heads and twitching their ears, the kittens kept their eyes shut tight as they imagined each magical note cascading around them. Sofia would nestle against Horatio, their tails intertwined and swinging in time with the music.

Jimmy always sat in the last row. He admired the bright red uniforms and tall black hats with elegant blue feathers. Led by Jimmy, the people in the audience would clap extra loudly after each melody so the musicians would know that they still appreciated hearing the beautiful music.

One evening, a man entered the hall wearing a dark hat that shadowed his face. "What brings you here tonight?" Jimmy asked him. Horatio, who had been patrolling the concert hall, hid under a nearby table and listened quietly.

"You've been doing a wonderful job," the man said, "but I have some bad news. Since so few people come to hear the orchestra play, the landlords have decided to close the concert hall. It will be torn down and replaced with a parking lot.

"I love this old place," Jimmy said, anxiously looking around the hall. "Is there any way to change their minds?"

"The final performance will be on Friday," said the man with the dark hat. "But if the hall is filled with people that evening, the landlords might change their minds. Do you think you can do that?"

When Jimmy quietly looked down, the man shook his head. "Then I think you'd better pack your bags and look for another place to live and work. We will be back on Friday to lock up the concert hall for good."

As Jimmy rubbed a tear from his eye, Horatio ran to tell his family the sad news. When he finished, Sofia asked, "Is there any way we can help?"

Horatio closed his eyes and thought really hard, but no ideas came. After whispering excitedly to each other, Mary and Eddie shouted, "We have an idea! Let's talk to all the pets and ask them to bring their owners to the concert hall on Friday evening."

"Yes!" Sofia smiled. "That is just what we must do. Let's ask all the cats and dogs to help us. If the hall is filled with people, those mean landlords will have to keep it open."

That night, the little family was almost too excited to sleep as they thought about their plan to save the concert hall.

Early the next morning, Mary and Eddie jumped on their parents to wake them up. They couldn't wait to start their important mission.

Horatio and Eddie went to the dog park, where Petie the Pug and a few other friends were playing games. The dogs all agreed to bring their owners to the concert hall on Friday evening and said they would tell their friends too.

Petie the Pug knew that the best way to spread the news was to see his friend Bruno, whose owner ran the newsstand under the train tracks. Bruno saw many pets each day as their owners bought newspapers and magazines. After the mission was explained, Bruno promised to tell all the animals who came by.

Sofia and Mary went to nearby beauty salons, where women were having their hair styled and nails polished. While the ladies were under the hair dryers, Sofia and Mary talked with their pets about the plan to save the concert hall.

On Friday, the family visited nearby supermarkets and spoke with many pets who were waiting outside or wandering down the aisles with their owners. Then they ran all the way across town to the shopping malls, where they found many pets walking on the concourses or in the stores. All the animals agreed to come to the concert hall that evening and to continue spreading the message.

Sofia and Mary saw two beautiful ladies carrying kittens in their bags. At their feet were Mimi, a small Chihuahua, and Buster, a petite Terrier. When the animals heard about saving the concert hall, they immediately offered to help.

Exhausted by their efforts, Horatio, Sofia, and the kittens returned to the concert hall late Friday afternoon and immediately fell fast asleep. They awoke to the familiar sounds of the musicians tuning their instruments. The orchestra was preparing to play for what could be the final performance.

After eating the special dinner that Jimmy brought up to the attic, the cats climbed onto his lap and snuggled close against him. Smiling sadly, he held each of them tightly while the orchestra prepared to play for the last time.

As Horatio, Sofia, and the kittens took their seats in the rafters, they saw Jimmy standing by the exit with his small battered suitcase.

The time had come for their final performance. Looking so handsome in their bright red uniforms and tall black hats, the musicians quietly took their seats on the stage. Seeing that only a few people had come, the conductor gave a heavy sigh and raised his white baton. This signaled for the tuba player to fill his cheeks and begin the first piece, which started with a deep, sad note.

Suddenly, a great racket could be heard outside the concert hall. Dogs were barking, cats were meowing, and people were shouting. When the musicians went to the windows, Mary and Eddie ran to the large attic window, with Horatio and Sofia close behind.

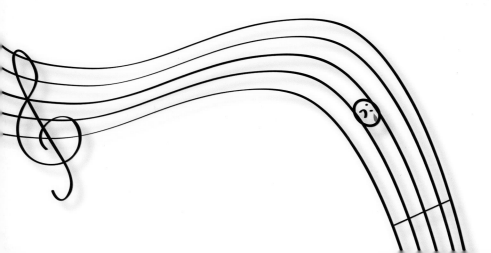

What a sight they saw! Pouring down the streets and sidewalks from every direction were dogs of every size, pulling their owners behind them. Cats of all colors were being chased by women with sparkly nails.

Bruno the German Shepherd led the crowd. Danny the Great Dane was pulling so hard that his owner's hat blew off and landed on a lady's new hairdo.

The doors burst open. Meowing cats, howling dogs, and surprised people filled the aisles. "Look everybody!" someone shouted. "The orchestra is about to play. Let's sit down and listen." Soon, all the seats were packed with people and pets.

The conductor looked over his shoulder and could not believe his eyes! With a huge smile, he waved his white baton, and the musicians burst into a high-spirited melody. Horatio, Sofia, and the kittens were overjoyed as they ran back to their seats. Their tails swished even more than usual as the merry, uplifting music filled the air.

When the man with the dark hat and the grumpy landlords entered the concert hall, their mouths dropped open and their eyes nearly popped out of their heads with shock. The orchestra had just finished the first lively arrangement, and the crowd erupted into a thunderous applause.

"Where did all these people come from?" the man with the dark hat asked Jimmy.

"I don't know," Jimmy said, scratching his head, "but I'm sure glad they're here!"

When the performance ended, the cheerful people and their pets began to leave. Laughing and humming the melodies, they were excited to tell all their friends about their wonderful evening at the concert hall. The landlords had big smiles, too, and they immediately decided that the hall would stay open after all. The orchestra would continue to play!

As Jimmy the Janitor heard the good news, he looked up at Horatio, Sofia, and the kittens. With a tear in his eye, he winked at them. Jimmy was sure he saw them wink back.

There are no endings, just new beginnings.

We hope *The Concert Hall Cats* will inspire everyone to embrace the arts, live musical performances, and historic buildings by supporting their local theaters, museums, landmark societies, and historical preservation efforts.

We hope this book reminds us to take care of all animals, because in their own special way animals take care of us.

Fausta, Michael and Joseph

Fausta and Michael McDermott are attorneys who practice together in Westchester County, New York. They have dedicated *The Concert Hall Cats* to their first two children, Stephanie and Anthony, who passed away as infants. Endeavoring to create something together that would bring joy to children, Fausta and Michael wrote the initial version of this sweet story in 1991. The grateful couple was eventually blessed with four healthy sons, Joseph, William and twins, John and Philip.

During high school, Joseph McDermott demonstrated artistic gifts, which have been developed and honed through the patient instruction of artist Alan Reingold. Joseph wanted to help his parents realize their dream of sharing *The Concert Hall Cats* with many children, so he spent several summers illustrating this story of love, hope, and survival.

Joseph is majoring in Peace Studies and Conflict Resolution (B.A., Class of 2015) at Manhattan College. Situated in Riverdale, New York, Manhattan College is also the *alma mater* of Michael (B.A., Class of 1981) and Fausta (B.A., Class of 1982).

Photo Credit: Alan Zale
AlanZale.com

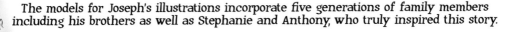

The models for Joseph's illustrations incorporate five generations of family members including his brothers as well as Stephanie and Anthony, who truly inspired this story.

Beautiful Tree Publishers, Inc.
293 Route 100
Suite 210
Somers, NY 10589
Tel: 914-276-2747
www.BeautifulTreePublishers.com

Gratitude for our models: We want to thank our family and friends who were models for the characters, including: Antonio Locorotondo (Jimmy); John McDermott (conductor); Stella Locorotondo and Theresa McDermott (ladies in salon); Lucia Girolamo and Fausta McDermott (ladies walking); Michael McDermott (the man in the dark hat); William McDermott (boy chasing dog); Alan Reingold (newsstand owner); Joseph McDermott (newsstand customer); John McDermott, Philip McDermott, Mary Fette, Ann Brennan, Patty McDermott, Kathy McDermott, Lucy Locorotondo, and our many nieces, nephews, and cousins (audience and chase scenes).

Gratitude for our editors: We want to thank the following members of the Illumination Arts team for their painstaking help in editing and polishing our story: John and Kim Thompson, Sara Kraft, Breanna Powell, Aysha Rafiq, Julia Saxby, Sarah Love, Kim Shealy, and Kelly Grant. Additional editing help was provided by Maria and Gordon Smith. Many thanks to Andrew F. Young, Esq. of Lackenbach Siegel LLP www.LSLLP.com for assistance with copyright matters.

ISBN: 978-0-9855417-7-4
First printing 2015
Published in the United States of America
Printed in China by Shanghai Chenxi Printing Co., Ltd.
Book Designer: Breanna Powell Design, Maple Valley, WA